This book belongs to

_____

_____

Copyright © 2012 Disney Enterprises, Inc.
All rights reserved.
For more information address
D𝒾sn𝑒𝑦 PRESS
114 Fifth Avenue
New York, New York 10011-5690

Ages 3 and up

Produced in association with
Parragon Books Ltd, UK

Printed in China
T814-8359-7-12190
ISBN 978-1-4231-7486-8
First Edition
10 9 8 7 6 5 4 3 2 1

For more Disney Press fun, visit www.disneybooks.com

# Beauty and the Beast

**Disney PRESS**

New York

Once upon a time, in a faraway land, a handsome young prince lived in a shining castle. Although he had everything his heart desired, the prince was spoiled, selfish, and unkind.

An old beggar woman offered the prince a single rose in return for shelter, but the selfish prince refused.

Suddenly, the old woman turned into an enchantress! She had seen that there was no love in the prince's heart. She turned him into a beast and placed a spell on the entire castle.

For the spell to be broken, the prince had to fall in love, and be loved in return. If it did not happen before the last petal fell from her rose, he would remain a beast forever.

Not far away, a young woman named Belle had her nose in a book. She loved to read, which seemed very strange to the local townspeople. Belle was also very beautiful, which made Gaston, the village's most handsome man, want to marry her.

Belle had no intention of marrying Gaston. She found him boorish and boring, and he didn't appreciate her love of books.

"It's not right for a woman to read," Gaston said. "Soon she gets ideas, starts thinking."

Belle rolled her eyes.

"Hey, what do you say you come and have a look at my hunting trophies?" Gaston said.

"Maybe some other time," Belle replied. "I have to get home and help my father."

Back at home, Belle's father, Maurice, waved to her as he and their horse, Phillipe, set out for the fair with his latest invention. Belle knew that the townspeople thought Maurice and his inventions were odd, but she believed in him with all her heart.

"Good-bye, Papa, good luck," Belle said as she waved.

As it got dark, Maurice and Phillipe got lost in the
woods and became separated. Suddenly, Maurice was
surrounded by snarling wolves! The pack chased Maurice
until they cornered him in front of a tall iron gate.

Thinking quickly, Maurice shook the gates open
and slipped behind them. In front of him, he saw an
enormous, gloomy castle.

To his surprise, the castle was full of charming, enchanted servants! Lumiere the candlestick and Cogsworth the clock ushered Maurice to a warm seat by the fire.

"What service!" Maurice exclaimed, both delighted and shocked by what he was seeing.

Suddenly, a strong gust of wind swept into the room, and extinguished Lumiere's flames and the fire in the fireplace. A frightening figure entered the room.

"So, you've come to stare?" shouted the Beast.

"I meant no harm," Maurice stammered. "I needed a place to stay."

"I'll give you a place to stay," replied the Beast. Then he locked Maurice in the dungeon!

Meanwhile, Gaston had decided it was his and Belle's wedding day. He had set up the perfect garden wedding and had gathered the village for the big event.

"I'd better go in there and . . . propose to the girl!" Gaston laughed.

Inside the cottage, Belle was sitting in a chair reading a book. There was a knock at the door.

"Say you'll marry me," Gaston said.

"I'm very sorry, Gaston, but I don't deserve you," Belle replied, showing him out.

Gaston was furious.

Soon afterwards, Phillipe returned home—alone.

"Phillipe, what are you doing here? Where's Papa?" Belle cried, greatly alarmed.

She grabbed her cape and told Phillipe to take her to her father. The horse led her to an enormous, old castle.

"What is this place?" she asked. She found her father's hat on the ground, so Belle bravely approached the castle doors.

Finally, Belle located Maurice in the dungeon. They tried to hug through the bars.

"Belle, I want you to leave this place," said Maurice. "No time to explain, you must go now!"

Belle refused to leave her father. Suddenly, the Beast grabbed Belle's shoulder and whipped her around.

"What are you doing here?" he growled.

"I've come for my father. Please let him out! Can't you see he's sick?" It was dark in the dungeon, and Belle could not see who was keeping her father captive.

"There's nothing you can do. He's my prisoner," the Beast growled.

"Take me, instead!" she bravely suggested.

The Beast accepted, with one condition. Belle had to promise to stay forever.

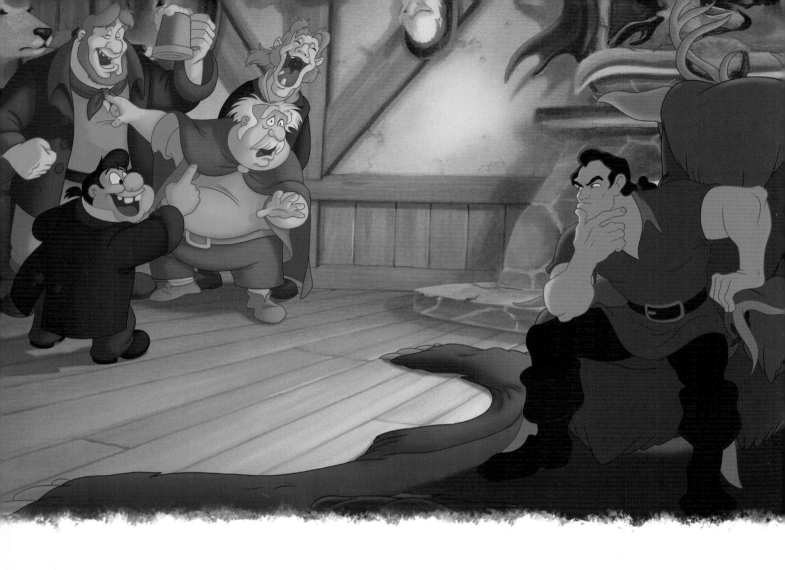

When Maurice returned to town, he begged for help to rescue Belle. The villagers asked who had taken her.

"A horrible, monstrous Beast!" shouted Maurice. But everyone just laughed at "crazy old Maurice."

Gaston began to think about how this turn of events could force Belle to marry him.

Back at the castle, Belle met Mrs. Potts and some of the others who lived there.

"That was a very brave thing you did, my dear," said Mrs. Potts. She knew that Belle had chosen to live in the castle in order to save Maurice.

"But I've lost my father, my dreams, everything," Belle said sadly.

That night, Belle refused to dine with the Beast.
Later, when she became hungry, she crept down to
the kitchen.

The staff treated her to a singing, dancing feast!
They were thrilled to finally have a guest.

After dinner, Belle went exploring. The Beast had
forbidden her to go into the castle's West Wing, but she
couldn't help being curious.

The dark rooms were filled with broken furniture and
mirrors. Belle noticed a shredded portrait in the corner
of the room. She lifted the pieces back into place and
revealed the face of a handsome man. Then Belle spotted
a beautiful rose, glowing under a glass dome. Several
petals lay near the stem.

Belle removed the dome and reached for the flower, but suddenly the Beast burst into the room. He grabbed the rose protectively.

"I warned you never to come here," he bellowed. "Do you know what you could have done?!"

Furiously, the Beast began to break things and screamed at the top of his voice, "GET OUT! GET OUT!"

In total fear, Belle fled the West Wing. She grabbed her cloak and ran down the stairs.

"Promise or no promise, I can't stay here another minute!" Belle cried. She ran in tears from the castle.

Belle climbed onto Phillipe, who was waiting outside, and rode away. Soon, they were surrounded by wolves. Belle rode Phillipe as best she could, but the wolves kept attacking.

The wolves were about to drag Belle away when the Beast arrived. Roaring, he lunged at the animals, shaking off their ferocious jaws and hurling them to the ground. Finally, the pack fled into the dark woods. One of the wolves had injured the Beast's arm.

Once they got back to the castle, Belle tried to tend to the Beast's wounds.

"If you hadn't run away, this wouldn't have happened," the Beast said.

"If you hadn't frightened me, I wouldn't have run away," Belle countered. Then she added, "By the way, thank you for saving my life."

"You're welcome," the Beast replied, gently.

Back in the village, Gaston met with Monsieur D'Arque from the Asylum de Loons. Gaston bribed D'Arque, instructing him to declare that Maurice was insane. Belle's father would be locked up in the asylum . . . unless Belle agreed to marry Gaston.

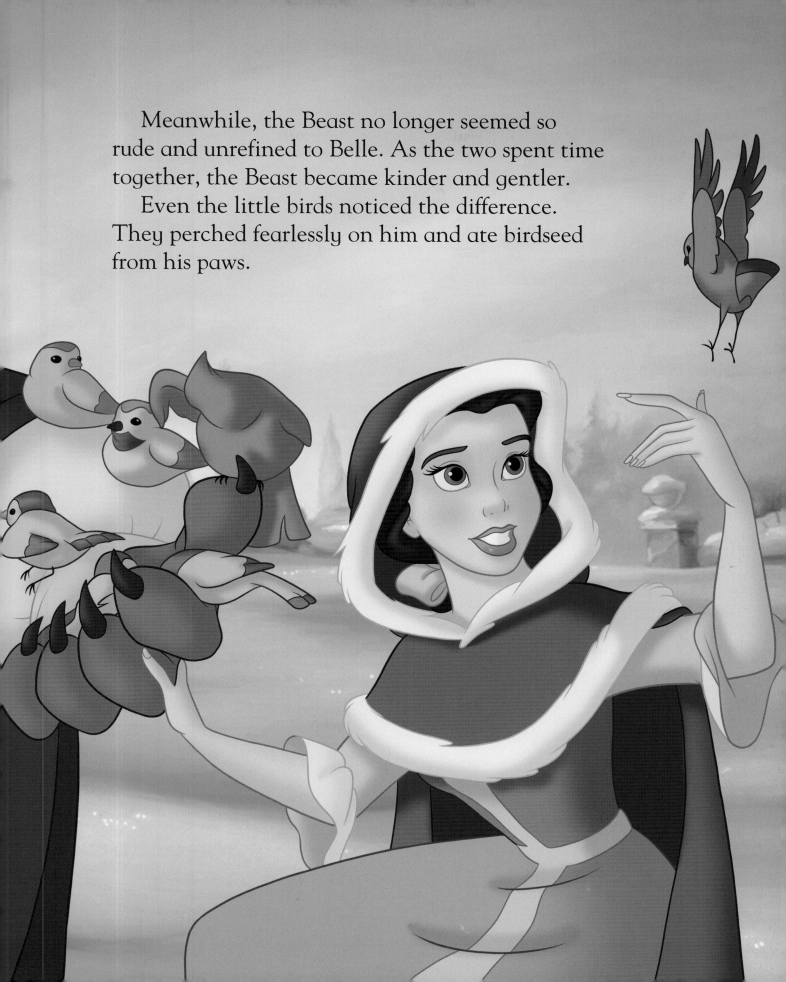

Meanwhile, the Beast no longer seemed so
rude and unrefined to Belle. As the two spent time
together, the Beast became kinder and gentler.
    Even the little birds noticed the difference.
They perched fearlessly on him and ate birdseed
from his paws.

The Beast arranged an elegant dinner
for himself and Belle. Lumiere and the other
servants hoped the two would declare their
love and break the spell.
After dinner, Belle and the Beast
entered the ballroom. They felt a little
awkward at first, but soon they were
whirling together across the floor.

Belle felt happy, but she missed her father. The Beast showed her an enchanted mirror, which revealed an image of her father. Maurice looked ill, and Belle knew he needed help.

There was only one petal left on the rose, but the Beast selflessly released Belle so she could go home to her father.

Soon after Belle arrived in the village, Gaston and the townspeople appeared. They hauled Maurice off to the asylum wagon, while Gaston explained his proposition to Belle, but she refused. She would never marry Gaston!

Belle told everyone her father wasn't crazy and proved it by showing them the Beast's image on the enchanted mirror.

Gaston sensed that Belle had feelings for the creature. Angry and jealous, Gaston led the townspeople toward the castle.

"I say we kill the Beast!" he shouted.

The townspeople marched up toward the castle, rammed the castle doors, and stormed into the building. The enchanted objects—the servants—defended the castle with all their might. The hat rack threw punches, the wardrobe fought back with her doors, and a bucket flung itself against the invaders.

Gaston slipped away to find the Beast for himself.

Gaston found the Beast. The Beast was already weak. He had been heartsick from missing Belle and had refused to fight back when the villagers attacked.

Outside on the balcony, the Beast saw that Belle had tried to come back and help him, and he reached for her.

Gaston saw his chance and stabbed him in the back! But as he did so, Gaston lost his grip on the railing and plunged to the ground.

"At least I got to see you one last time," the Beast told Belle, after Gaston was finally defeated. The Beast closed his eyes and fell back, his body still.

Belle began to cry as she hugged herself tightly to the Beast.

"No, no! Please don't leave me," Belle sobbed. "I love you!"

There was a moment of silence. Then suddenly, light shone down onto the Beast and his body rose into the air. Belle watched, amazed, as the Beast twisted around and transformed into . . .

. . . a handsome prince!

"Belle," he said softly. "It's me."

Belle looked up into his eyes. "It is you!" she cried, in wonder.

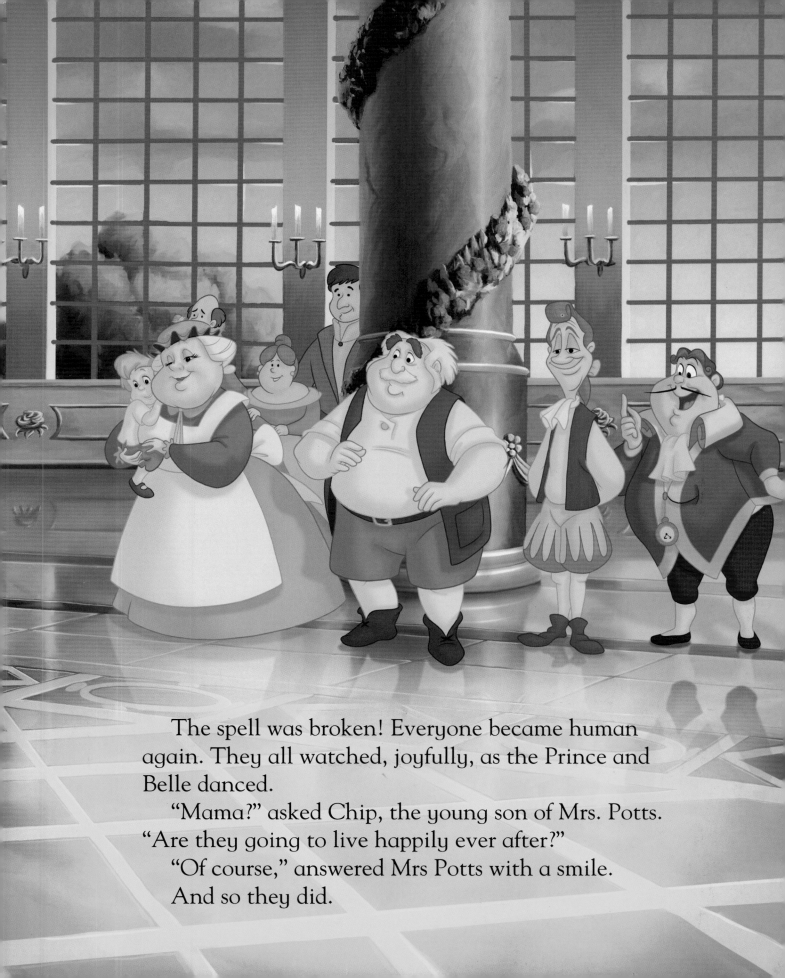

The spell was broken! Everyone became human again. They all watched, joyfully, as the Prince and Belle danced.

"Mama?" asked Chip, the young son of Mrs. Potts. "Are they going to live happily ever after?"

"Of course," answered Mrs Potts with a smile.

And so they did.

The End